A CHRISTMAS PROMISE OF LOVE

KAYLA LOWE

Copyright © 2024 by Kayla Lowe

All rights reserved.

No part of this book may be reproduced in any form or by any electronic or mechanical means, including information storage and retrieval systems, without written permission from the author, except for the use of brief quotations in a book review.

Want a free book? Sign up to my newsletter to get my award-winning book for free! www.authorkaylalowe.com

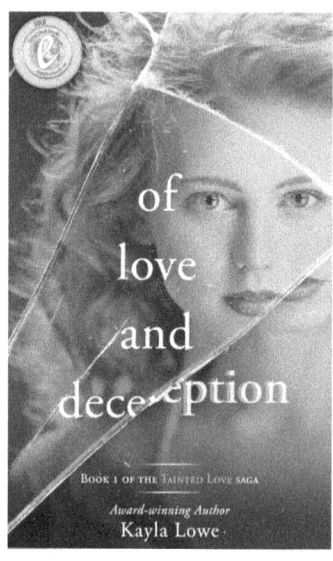

MORE OF MY BOOKS

Series

Women of the Bible Fiction

Ruth
Esther
Rachel
Hannah
Deborah

Charms of the Chaste Court

A Courtship in Covent Garden
Whispers in Westminster
Romance in Regent's Park
Serenade on Strand Street
Treasure in Tower Bridge

Sweet Honey by the Sea

The Beekeeper's Secret (Book 1)
A Royal Honeycomb (Book 2)
Bees in Blossom (Book 3)

Honeyed Kisses (Book 4)
Blooming Forever (Book 5)

Strawberry Beach Series

Beachside Lessons (Book 1)
Beachside Lessons (Book 2)
Beachside Lessons (Book 3)

Panama City Beach Series

Sun-Kissed Secrets (Book 1)
Sun-Kissed Secrets (Book 2)
Sun-Kissed Secrets (Book 3)

The Tainted Love Saga

Of Love and Deception (Book 1)
Of Love and Family (Book 2)
Of Love and Violence (Book 3)
Of Love and Abuse (Book 4)
Of Love and Crime (Book 5)
Of Love and Addiction (Book 6)
Of Love and Redemption (Book 7)

Standalones

Maiden's Blush

Poetry

Phantom Poetry
Lost and Found

1

Emily finished hanging the last of the glittery snowflake ornaments on the towering evergreen in the town square. She stepped back to admire her handiwork, the twinkling lights reflecting in her warm brown eyes. Around her, the small town bustled with holiday cheer as people hurried about, arms laden with shopping bags and faces rosy from the crisp December air.

Despite the festive atmosphere, a familiar pang of loneliness crept into Emily's heart. Another Christmas season alone. She sighed, her breath forming a frosty cloud.

"Lord, I know your timing is perfect," she

whispered, pulling her knitted scarf tighter. "But I can't help feeling this emptiness. Please, show me your plan."

As if in answer, a friendly voice called out from behind her. "Emily Parkins, is that you?"

Startled, Emily spun around, her chestnut waves bouncing. Her eyes widened as recognition dawned. "Luke Reynolds?"

The handsome man grinned, his blue eyes crinkling at the corners. He looked different from the lanky teen she remembered, now broad-shouldered and rugged. But his kind smile was the same.

"I almost didn't recognize you without pigtails," Luke teased, pulling her into a warm hug. The scent of pine and winter surrounded them.

Emily laughed as they parted, her cheeks flushed. "And I almost didn't recognize you without grass stains on your jeans from all our adventures. When did you get back in town?"

"Just last week. It's good to be home." Luke's gaze turned wistful for a moment before brightening again. "I heard you're a teacher now. Those kids are lucky to have you."

Pride swelled in Emily's chest. "I love what I do. Shaping young hearts and minds is a true privilege." She tilted her head. "What about you? How long are you in town for?"

Luke shrugged, hands in his pockets. "Indefinitely, I suppose. I'm still figuring out my next steps now that my mission work is done."

As they talked and laughed, catching up on the years apart, Emily marveled at how easy it was to be in Luke's presence again. Like no time had passed at all. An unfamiliar flutter stirred in her heart.

Around them, the town continued its cheerful preparations. Children's laughter mingled with Christmas carols as volunteers strung more lights and hung wreaths. Emily breathed in the festive air, a contented smile on her lips. Maybe, just maybe, God did have a plan unfolding before her eyes this holiday season.

The church stood at the heart of the town, its stained glass windows casting a kaleidoscope of colors across the snow-dusted steps. Emily climbed them with a box of decorations in her arms, the warmth of the sanctuary enveloping her as she stepped inside.

Setting the box down, she began to sort through the glittering ornaments and garlands, her mind still lingering on her conversation with Luke. It had been so long since they'd seen each other, yet the connection between them seemed as strong as ever. She couldn't help but wonder what God had in store.

As she reached for the next decoration, her hand brushed against the worn leather of her Bible. Emily paused, a gentle smile tugging at her lips as she lifted it from the box. The pages fell open to a well-loved passage, a small piece of paper fluttering to the ground.

Curious, Emily bent to retrieve it. The note was faded and creased, but the words were still clear, written in her own teenage handwriting:

> Trust in the Lord with all your heart, and lean not on your own understanding. — Proverbs 3:5

Memories flooded back—a younger Emily,

scribbling those words as a promise to herself, to trust God's timing in matters of the heart. She'd been so eager for love then, so certain that God would bring the right person into her life at the perfect moment.

Years had passed, and that moment hadn't come. But as Emily stood there, holding the note and reflecting on her chance meeting with Luke, a flicker of hope ignited in her heart. Perhaps she'd been too focused on her own understanding, too caught up in the loneliness to see the bigger picture.

With a deep breath, Emily closed her eyes and whispered a prayer. "Lord, I surrender my heart to Your timing once again. Help me to trust in Your plan, even when I can't see the path ahead."

As she opened her eyes, a sense of peace washed over her. The loneliness that had felt so heavy suddenly seemed lighter, as if a burden had been lifted. Emily tucked the note back into her Bible, a reminder of the promise she'd made and the faith she held onto.

With renewed energy, she turned back to the box of decorations, eager to transform the church into a celebration of joy and hope. As she worked, Emily's thoughts drifted to Luke, and the unexpected warmth his presence had brought. Only God knew what the future held, but for now, she was content to live in this moment, surrounded by the love of her community and the promise of His plan.

2

The bell above the café door jingled as Emily stepped inside, the warm aroma of coffee and freshly baked muffins enveloping her. She stamped the snow from her boots, her eyes scanning the cozy interior. Her heart skipped a beat when she spotted a familiar figure at the counter—sandy blonde hair, broad shoulders, a flannel shirt she'd recognize anywhere.

Luke turned, and their eyes met. A slow smile spread across his face, lighting up those striking blue eyes. He waved her over.

She felt a flutter in her chest as she neared him. He stood as she approached, and they shared a quick, slightly awkward hug. "Fancy seeing you here," she murmured.

"Do you come here often?" He asked as he rubbed the back of his neck.

Emily nodded. "Oh yes, they have the best coffees in town."

They got their coffees and settled at a small table by the frosted window. Emily warmed her hands on her mug, sneaking glances at Luke. He seemed different somehow—older, wiser, but still with that kind sparkle in his eye. She said a silent prayer, asking for guidance in navigating these unexpected feelings.

"So, tell me about your mission trips," Emily prompted. "I'd love to hear about your experiences."

Luke's face lit up as he began to share stories—the communities he helped build, the faith he witnessed in the face of adversity. "It was humbling, you know? Seeing how God works in people's lives, even in the darkest of times."

Emily listened intently, inspired by the passion in his voice. She could see how much he had grown, how deeply his faith ran. It stirred something in her own heart, a longing for that same sense of purpose.

"But now," Luke continued, "I feel like I'm in a new chapter. Waiting for God to show me the next step." He met her gaze, and Emily felt a spark of understanding pass between them.

"I know what you mean," she said softly. "Sometimes it's hard to be patient, to trust in His timing." Her thoughts drifted to her own hopes and dreams, the unspoken desires of her heart.

Luke reached across the table and gave her hand a gentle squeeze. "But that's where faith comes in, right? Trusting even when we can't see the full picture."

Emily smiled, warmed by his reassurance. As they continued to catch up, laughter and memories mingling with the clink of coffee cups, she couldn't help but wonder if this unexpected reunion was part of God's plan all along.

As their conversation began to wind down, Luke leaned forward, a hopeful glint in his eye. "Actually, Emily, I wanted to ask you something."

Emily's heart skipped a beat, her fingers curling around her coffee mug. "What is it, Luke?"

"Well, the church is holding a community outreach event for Christmas, helping families in need." He smiled, his face lighting up with enthusiasm. "We're putting together care packages, organizing a toy drive, even planning a special holiday meal. And I thought, well, I wondered if you might like to join me?"

Emily blinked, surprised by the invitation. "Oh, Luke, that sounds wonderful." She could picture it already, working side by side with him, bringing joy to those less fortunate. It was exactly the kind of thing that filled her heart with purpose.

"I'd love to help," she said, smiling warmly. "Just tell me what you need me to do."

Luke grinned, his relief evident. "That's great, Emily. I knew I could count on you." He pulled out his phone, scrolling through the details. "We're meeting at the church on Saturday morning to start putting everything together. I can pick you up if you'd like?"

Emily nodded, trying to ignore the flutter in her stomach at the thought of spending more time with him. "That would be perfect, thank you."

As they exchanged numbers and made plans, Emily couldn't help but notice the nervous energy that hummed between them. It was like a current, a pull that drew them together despite the years apart. She wondered if Luke felt it too, this sense that something more was happening, just beneath the surface.

But for now, she focused on the task at hand, the opportunity to make a difference in their community. It was a chance to put her faith into action, to show God's love in a tangible way. And if it meant spending more time with Luke, well, that was just an added blessing.

3

Emily's breath clouded in the crisp December air as she handed a brightly wrapped gift to a wide-eyed little girl. The child's grateful smile warmed her heart, chasing away the chill. Beside her, Luke handed out packages of food, his blue eyes shining with the same joy she felt.

"You're a natural at this," Luke said, flashing Emily a grin. "The kids love you."

She laughed softly. "I love doing this. Seeing their faces light up...it's what Christmas is all about."

They worked in comfortable silence for a while, the only sounds the delighted chatter of children and the rustle of wrapping paper. Emily couldn't help but admire Luke's gentle way with the families, how he took time to listen to each person's story.

During a lull, they found themselves side by side again, taking a moment to catch their breath. Luke's gaze held a faraway look, a melancholy Emily recognized.

"The holidays haven't been the same since I lost my parents," he confided quietly. "Being here, giving back...it helps, but the ache is still there, you know?"

Emily laid a comforting hand on his arm. "I understand. Loneliness has a way of magnifying grief, especially this time of year."

Luke met her eyes, a flicker of vulnerability in his expression. "How do you manage it?"

She smiled gently. "Prayer, mostly. Trusting that God has a plan, even when I can't see it. It's not always easy, but my faith keeps me going."

He nodded slowly. "I admire your strength, Emily. Your unwavering hope."

A blush crept into her cheeks at the sincere compliment. Before she could respond, a volunteer called for their help distributing the last of the gifts.

As they rejoined the bustle of activity, Emily

felt a newfound connection to Luke, a shared understanding borne of their mutual struggles and faith. She sent up a silent prayer, grateful for this moment of bonding and the reminder that even in the depths of loneliness, God always provided comfort and companionship.

As the last gifts were handed out and grateful families departed, Emily and Luke found themselves lingering in the now-quiet community center. The twinkling Christmas lights cast a warm glow over their tired but contented faces.

"I can't thank you enough for all your help today, Luke," Emily said softly as she turned to face him. "Seeing the joy on those children's faces...it's moments like these that remind me why I love teaching so much."

Luke smiled, his blue eyes crinkling at the corners. "It's been a privilege to work alongside you, Emily. Your dedication to your students and this community is truly inspiring."

A comfortable silence settled between them as they began tidying up the space. Emily's mind drifted to their earlier conversation, the vulnerability they had shared. She felt a tug in her heart, a longing to connect with Luke on a deeper level.

Almost as if he sensed her thoughts, Luke spoke up. "Emily, would you...would you mind if we prayed together before we leave? I feel like God has been stirring something in my heart today, and I'd love to lift it up to Him with you."

Surprised but pleased, Emily nodded. "I would love that, Luke."

They found a quiet corner and clasped hands, bowing their heads in reverence. Luke's voice, usually so steady, wavered with emotion as he began to pray.

"Heavenly Father, we come before you tonight with hearts full of gratitude. Thank you for the opportunity to serve these families and to experience the true joy of giving. Lord, I ask that you continue to guide Emily and me as we navigate this season of our lives. Help us to trust in your plan, even when the path ahead is unclear."

Emily squeezed his hand gently, her own heart swelling with affection and faith. She continued the prayer, her voice a soothing balm.

"God, I pray that you would heal the wounds of the past and fill any emptiness with your love. Give us the courage to open our hearts to the blessings you have in store. May we always remember that with you, we are never truly alone."

As they whispered "Amen" in unison, Emily and Luke lifted their heads, eyes meeting in a moment of profound connection. The air between them seemed to hum with a new energy, a budding affection that both thrilled and terrified them.

Luke cleared his throat, reluctantly releasing Emily's hands. "Thank you for praying with me, Emily. It means more than you know."

She smiled softly, her brown eyes warm with understanding. "Anytime, Luke. I'm here for you, always."

As they gathered their belongings and prepared to part ways, both Emily and Luke couldn't shake the feeling that this night had been a turning point. A seed of love, planted by shared faith and nurtured by compassion, had taken root in their hearts. Though neither was ready to voice it aloud, they knew that God was weaving their paths together in a beautiful tapestry of His design.

With a final exchange of gentle goodnights, Emily and Luke stepped out into the crisp winter air, their souls warmed by the knowledge that they had found a kindred spirit in each other. The future, though uncertain, held the promise of love guided by a shared faith that would see them through any challenge that lay ahead.

4

Emily's fingers hesitated over the keys, her eyes fixed on the doorbell that had just sounded through her quiet home. She wasn't expecting anyone this evening. Setting aside her laptop, she made her way to the front door and opened it. Her breath caught in her throat.

"Ryan?" The name fell from her lips, barely above a whisper.

"Hi Em." Her ex boyfriend's familiar lopsided grin greeted her, though it didn't quite reach his eyes. "Can I come in?"

Wordlessly, she stepped aside, allowing him to enter. As he brushed past, the faint scent of his cologne—the same one he'd worn when they were together—stirred memories she'd long since packed away.

"What are you doing here?" She found her voice, closing the door and turning to face him.

Ryan ran a hand through his hair, a gesture she once found endearing. "I'm back in town for a while. I was hoping we could talk, maybe catch up?"

Emily folded her arms across her chest, a subconscious shield. "It's been a long time, Ryan. Why now?"

He took a step closer, his eyes searching hers. "I've been thinking about us a lot lately. About how things ended. I realized...I made a mistake letting you go."

Her heart squeezed, old feelings rising unbidden. But along with them came a gentle whisper, a reminder of the peace she'd found in trusting God's plan. She took a deep breath.

"Ryan, I appreciate you coming here, but I've moved on. I believe God has closed that chapter for us."

His brow furrowed. "Just like that? You're not even willing to try again?"

She shook her head gently. "It's not about trying. It's about trusting in something bigger than ourselves. I wish you all the best, truly. But I know this isn't the path for me anymore."

Ryan's shoulders sagged, disappointment etched on his features. "I see. Well, I guess I should go then." He moved towards the door, pausing with his hand on the knob. "Take care of yourself, Em."

And then he was gone, leaving Emily with a swirl of emotions and the unwavering knowledge that she'd done the right thing.

The next morning, Emily found herself at the local coffee shop, hands wrapped around a steaming mug as she waited for Luke. Sunlight streamed through the frosted windows, casting a warm glow over the cozy interior. The rich aroma of freshly brewed coffee mingled with the sweet scent of cinnamon rolls, a comforting familiarity that helped settle her nerves.

Luke arrived a few minutes later, the bell above the door announcing his presence. He spotted her immediately, his blue eyes crinkling at the corners as he smiled. He made his way over, shrugging off his coat and draping it over the back of the chair before sitting down.

"Good morning," he greeted warmly. "I hope you haven't been waiting long."

Emily shook her head, returning his smile. "Not at all. I'm just glad we could meet up. There's something I wanted to talk to you about."

Luke's brow furrowed slightly, concern flickering in his gaze. "Is everything alright?"

She took a deep breath, her fingers tightening around her mug. "Ryan came to see me last night. Out of the blue."

Luke stilled, his expression unreadable. "Your ex-boyfriend Ryan?"

Emily nodded. "He said he was back in town and wanted to catch up. But it was more than that. He..." She paused, gathering her thoughts. "He said he made a mistake letting me go. That he wanted to try again."

Silence stretched between them, the chatter of the other patrons fading into the background. Luke's jaw tightened almost imperceptibly, his gaze dropping to the untouched coffee in front of him.

"And what did you say?" His voice was carefully neutral.

"I told him that I've moved on. That I believe God has closed that chapter for us." Emily's words were soft but firm. "It wasn't easy, seeing him again after all this time. But I know in my heart that it's not the path meant for me."

Luke nodded slowly, his eyes still fixed on his coffee. The steam curled upwards, dissipating into the air between them. Emily watched him, her heart aching at the sudden distance she felt.

"Luke?" She reached out, her hand hovering hesitantly over his. "Are you alright?"

He finally looked up, meeting her gaze. There was a sadness in his eyes that she couldn't quite place, a vulnerability that he rarely allowed to surface.

"I'm glad you were able to find closure," he said quietly. "I know how much your faith means to you. How much you trust in God's plan."

Emily's fingers brushed against his, a feather-light touch.

"I knew you would understand." Emily smiled at him.

"What are friends for," he grinned back, though his smile didn't quite reach his eyes.

That evening, Emily found herself alone in her cozy living room, a soft blanket draped over her lap and her well-worn Bible resting in her hands. The events of the past two days swirled through her mind—Ryan's unexpected return, her heart-to-heart with Luke, the exhilarating promise of a new beginning.

She closed her eyes, breathing in the comforting scent of the vanilla candle flickering on the coffee table. Her heart was full, brimming with gratitude and awe at the way God worked in her life.

"Thank you," she whispered, her words carried heavenward on a sigh. "Thank you for Your guidance, for Your perfect timing. For bringing Luke into my life and showing me the beauty of Your plan."

The twinkling lights of the Christmas tree cast a warm glow across the room, but even their cheerful sparkle couldn't quite ease the turmoil in her heart.

She reached for her well-worn Bible on the side table, fingers tracing the familiar leather cover. She closed her eyes, taking a moment to center herself before opening to a random page. The words of Jeremiah 29:11 stared back at her:

> For I know the plans I have for you,
> declares the Lord, plans to
> prosper you and not to harm
> you, plans to give you hope and
> a future.

A soft smile played on her lips as she read the verse aloud, the words a balm to her troubled soul. "Lord," she whispered, "I come to you now, seeking your wisdom and guidance..."

As she prayed, images of Luke flooded her mind—his kind smile, the way his eyes crinkled when he laughed, the gentleness of his touch. Her heart swelled with affection, and suddenly, the confusion began to dissipate.

Closing her eyes once more, she continued her prayer.

Peace settled over her as she finished, a sense of calm washing away the day's anxieties. She knew that no matter what the future held, God would be by her side, guiding her every step.

With renewed faith, Emily hugged the Bible to her chest, a soft smile on her face. "Thank you," she whispered, "for your unending love and wisdom. I trust in you, now and always."

As she sat there, bathed in the soft glow of the Christmas lights, Emily felt a glimmer of hope. Whatever tomorrow brought, she knew she'd face it with God's strength and Luke's unwavering friendship. And for now, that was enough.

5

Emily wrapped her hands around the warm mug of tea, inhaling the fragrant steam as she sat across from Mrs. Evans in the church counseling room. Soft light filtered through the lace curtains, casting a gentle glow on the weathered oak table between them.

"I just don't know what to do," Emily confessed, meeting the older woman's compassionate gaze. "My heart yearns for Luke, but I'm afraid of ruining our friendship if he doesn't feel the same way."

Mrs. Evans reached out and patted Emily's hand. "My dear, God's timing is always perfect. Trust in His plan for you." She smiled knowingly.

"I've seen the way Luke looks at you. There's a special connection between you two."

Emily felt her cheeks warm. "You really think so?"

"I do. But rushing into things isn't always wise. Pray for guidance and have faith that if it's meant to be, God will open the right doors at the right time." Mrs. Evans' eyes twinkled with a hint of mischief. "In the meantime, keep being the wonderful friend and teacher you are. Your light shines brightly, Emily."

Across town, Luke paced the cramped pastor's office, running a hand through his sandy hair. Pastor Tom leaned back in his chair, listening intently as Luke poured out his heart.

"I care for Emily deeply," Luke admitted, his voice thick with emotion. "But I worry that pursuing a relationship now could complicate things. I've just returned home and I'm still finding my way."

Pastor Tom nodded thoughtfully. "It's understandable to have reservations, Luke. Your friendship with Emily is precious." He steepled his fingers, considering his next words carefully. "However, don't let fear hold you back from what could be a beautiful, God-ordained relationship."

Luke sank into the chair opposite the pastor, his brow furrowed. "I just don't want to risk losing her entirely if things don't work out."

"Have faith, son." Pastor Tom's voice was gentle but firm. "Trust in the Lord's guidance. If you and Emily are meant to be together, He will make a way. But you must also be willing to take a step forward in faith."

Luke let out a heavy sigh, knowing the pastor's words rang true. He closed his eyes for a moment, silently praying for wisdom and courage. When he opened them again, a glimmer of determination shone in their blue depths. Perhaps it was time to trust God and take a chance on love.

❄

The soft glow of candlelight illuminated the church sanctuary as Emily and Luke found their seats in the crowded pews. The air was filled with the scent of pine and cinnamon, and the gentle murmur of conversation hummed around them. Emily smoothed her burgundy skirt, her heart fluttering with a mixture of nerves and excitement at Luke's proximity.

As the first notes of "Silent Night" filled the room, Emily and Luke joined their voices with the congregation. Their harmonies blended seamlessly, creating a moment of shared reverence and connection. Emily felt a warmth bloom in her chest, a sense of peace and belonging washing over her.

Luke glanced at Emily, admiring the way the candlelight danced across her features. Her eyes were closed, lost in the music, and a small smile played on her lips. In that moment, Luke felt an overwhelming sense of rightness, as if God was whispering to his heart.

Leaning closer to Emily, Luke whispered, "Your voice is beautiful. I'm glad we could share this tradition together."

Emily's eyes fluttered open, meeting Luke's gaze. "Me too," she murmured, a faint blush coloring her cheeks. "There's something special about singing these carols. They always fill me with hope and joy."

As the service continued, Emily and Luke found themselves drawn into the spirit of the season. They exchanged smiles and knowing glances, their voices rising and falling in perfect unison. In the sanctuary's warmth and the glow of the candles, the rest of the world seemed to fade away, leaving only the two of them and the music.

I've never felt so connected to someone, Luke mused, his heart swelling with affection for the woman beside him. *It's as if our souls are singing in harmony.*

When the final carol came to a close, the congregation fell into a contented silence. Emily and Luke turned to each other, their eyes shining with the magic of the moment. In that instant, Luke knew that God was urging him to take a leap of faith.

"Emily," he began, his voice soft but earnest, "I was wondering if you might like to..."

6

Before Luke could finish his question, a familiar voice cut through their conversation.

"Emily, can I talk to you for a minute?" Ryan approached them, hands stuffed in his pockets, brow furrowed.

Emily's heart sank. She instinctively knew anything Ryan had to say wouldn't be good. Luke shifted uncomfortably beside her.

"One minute," Emily said gently but firmly. She glanced at Luke apologetically before she got up and stepped away with Ryan.

Luke knew he shouldn't eavesdrop, but he couldn't help straining to hear their conversation.

"Please, Em. Just give me a chance to explain,"

Ryan pleaded, taking a step closer. "I know we had our issues, but I really think we should try again."

Emily took a deep breath, summoning her courage. "I'm sorry, Ryan, but I've moved on. What we had is in the past now. I wish you all the best, truly, but my heart is leading me in a different direction."

She met his gaze steadily, willing him to understand. Ryan's shoulders slumped in defeat.

"I…I understand," he said quietly. "I hope you know I do want you to be happy, Em. I just had to try again. I won't bother you anymore. Take care of yourself." With a final nod, he turned and walked away, disappearing into the night.

Emily released a shaky breath she didn't realize she'd been holding. She walked back over to Luke. He placed a comforting hand on her shoulder.

"Are you alright?" he asked softly, concern etched on his handsome features.

Emily managed a small smile. "I will be. Thank you for being here, Luke. It means a lot."

He smiled warmly in return. "Always. Hey, it's getting late. Let me walk you home?"

Emily nodded gratefully. As they began the short trek to her house, gentle snowflakes began to drift down from the dark sky. The picturesque scene seemed to mirror the peace settling over Emily's heart. She knew closing the door on her past with Ryan was the right choice.

Luke cleared his throat, drawing her attention. "Emily, there's something I've been wanting to talk to you about," he began, his voice tinged with nervousness.

She glanced up at him curiously. In the amber glow of the streetlights, Luke's blue eyes shone with sincerity and...something more. Her pulse quickened.

"I've been doing a lot of praying and soul-searching lately," Luke continued, choosing his words carefully, "and I feel God is leading me to pursue...well, you. Us."

Emily's breath caught. Could this really be happening?

"I know our lives have taken different paths, but I can't ignore how I feel about you anymore," Luke said earnestly, taking her gloved hands in his. "You have the most beautiful heart, Emily, and I would be honored to have a chance to cherish it, if you'll let me."

Snowflakes dusted Luke's hair as he gazed at her hopefully, vulnerably. In that moment, Emily saw the answer to so many whispered prayers reflected in his eyes. A slow smile spread across her face.

"I would love nothing more," she whispered.

As they stood hand-in-hand amidst the swirling snow, Emily marveled at the beautiful scene God had painted. This felt like the beginning of a love story penned by the Author of her heart—one full of hope, faith, and the promise of forever.

❄

The twinkling Christmas lights cast a warm glow over the snow-covered street as Luke and Emily stood facing each other, their hearts full of newfound joy and possibility. Luke gently brushed a snowflake from Emily's cheek, his touch sending a shiver down her spine that had nothing to do with the cold.

"Emily," he said softly, his voice deep with emotion, "I promise to always honor your heart and our shared faith as we step into this relationship together. You deserve nothing less than a love that reflects Christ's own love for us."

Tears of happiness pricked at the corners of Emily's eyes. She had waited so long for this moment, trusting in God's perfect timing even when the loneliness felt overwhelming. Now, as she gazed into Luke's earnest blue eyes, she knew beyond a doubt that this was the answer to her prayers.

"I know you will," she replied, her voice barely above a whisper. "I've seen the depth of your faith and the kindness of your heart, Luke. I feel so blessed to have you in my life."

Luke's face broke into a wide, boyish grin that made Emily's heart skip a beat. He pulled her close, wrapping his arms around her as if he never wanted to let go. Emily melted into his embrace, savoring the feeling of being cherished and protected.

As they stood there, lost in each other's arms, the rest of the world seemed to fade away. The soft strains of a Christmas carol drifted from a nearby house, mingling with the gentle whisper of the falling snow. Emily closed her eyes, committing every detail of this perfect moment to memory.

When they finally pulled apart, Luke took Emily's hand in his, lacing their fingers together. "What do you say we get you home before you turn into a popsicle?" he teased, his eyes sparkling with mirth.

Emily laughed, feeling lighter and happier than she had in years. "Lead the way," she replied, squeezing his hand.

As they set off down the street, their footsteps leaving twin trails in the freshly fallen snow, Emily marveled at the unexpected twist her life had taken. She had a feeling that this was just the beginning of a beautiful adventure—one filled with love, laughter, and a faith that could move mountains.

And as the Christmas lights twinkled overhead, casting their magical glow over the snowy street, Emily knew that she was exactly where she was meant to be. In the arms of a man who loved her deeply, with a heart full of hope and a future bright with promise.

7

The warmth of Luke's hand enveloped Emily's as they strolled through the snow-covered church courtyard, their breaths mingling in frosty puffs. Twinkling lights adorned the trees, casting a golden glow on their smiling faces. Emily's heart swelled with joy, marveling at the love blossoming between them.

"I never thought I'd find someone who understands my heart like you do, Luke," Emily said softly, leaning into his shoulder. "It's like God brought us together at just the right time."

Luke squeezed her hand, his blue eyes reflecting the shimmering lights. "I feel the same way, Em. Being with you feels like coming home, like this is exactly where I'm meant to be."

They paused by the nativity scene, the figures of Mary and Joseph gazing adoringly at the baby Jesus. Emily felt a deep sense of peace wash over her. Just as God had orchestrated the greatest love story of all time, she knew He was weaving together her own beautiful tale with Luke.

As they entered the warm sanctuary, the scent of pine and cinnamon enveloped them. Familiar faces turned to greet the new couple, their smiles widening at the sight of Emily and Luke hand-in-hand.

"Emily, Luke, over here!" Emily's best friend Sarah waved from a nearby pew, patting the space beside her. "I saved you seats."

They settled in, exchanging hugs and holiday greetings with their church family. Emily closed her eyes for a moment, savoring the comforting sounds of gentle chatter and rustling coats. When she opened them, Luke was watching her with a tender smile.

"Penny for your thoughts?" he whispered, tucking a stray curl behind her ear.

Emily leaned into his touch, her heart full. "I was just thinking about how far God has brought me. Last year, I felt so alone and unsure. But now, surrounded by all this love and support, I know I was never truly alone. He was with me every step."

Luke nodded, understanding shining in his eyes. "And He brought us together, to walk this journey side by side."

As the service began, the first notes of "O Come All Ye Faithful" filling the air, Emily rested her head on Luke's shoulder. She knew that no matter what the future held, they would face it together, their love rooted in the unwavering faithfulness of God.

❄

The crisp night air enveloped Emily and Luke as they stepped out of the church, hand in hand. Twinkling lights adorned the trees lining the path, casting a warm glow over the freshly fallen snow. Luke's heart raced as he led her towards the gazebo, its wooden frame wrapped in garlands and ribbons.

"Luke, where are we going?" Emily laughed, her breath forming little clouds in the cold.

He smiled down at her, his blue eyes sparkling with anticipation. "You'll see. I have a surprise for you."

As they reached the gazebo, Emily gasped. Candles flickered on every surface, their soft light dancing across the intricate lattice work. Red rose petals were scattered across the floor, forming a heart at the center.

"Oh, Luke," she breathed, her eyes shining with tears. "It's beautiful."

Luke turned to face her, taking both of her hands in his. "Emily, from the moment I came back home, I knew God had led me to you. Your faith, your kindness, your unwavering hope—they've inspired me in ways I never thought possible."

He reached into his pocket, pulling out a small velvet box. Emily's hand flew to her mouth as he sank to one knee, opening the box to reveal a simple, elegant diamond ring.

"I promise to love you as deeply and unconditionally as God loves us both. I promise to be your partner in faith, to support you, cherish you, and grow with you." His voice wavered with emotion as he looked up at her, his heart in his eyes. "Emily Parkins, will you marry me?"

Tears streamed down Emily's face as she nodded, a joyful laugh bubbling up from her throat. "Yes, Luke, yes! A thousand times yes!"

He slipped the ring onto her finger, rising to pull her into a tight embrace. They clung to each other, swaying gently in the candlelight as the distant strains of "Joy to the World" echoed through the night.

Emily pulled back slightly, cupping Luke's face in her hands. "I know our love is a gift from God," she whispered, her eyes shining with certainty. "And I trust in His timing, His plan for us. I can't wait to spend the rest of my life with you, growing in faith and love."

Luke leaned down, capturing her lips in a tender kiss. As they lost themselves in the moment, snowflakes began to drift down from the sky, dusting their hair and shoulders like a heavenly blessing. They laughed, tilting their heads back to catch the flakes on their tongues, their hearts overflowing with the joy and peace of God's love.

Hand in hand, they made their way back towards the church, ready to share their happiness with their loved ones. Emily glanced down at her ring, the diamond glittering in the soft light. She knew that this was just the beginning of their journey together, a journey guided by faith, trust, and the unshakable foundation of God's eternal love.

8

The joyous laughter of family and friends filled the cozy living room, enveloping Emily and Luke in a warm embrace. Twinkling lights from the Christmas tree danced in their eyes as they held hands, their new engagement rings glinting in the soft glow.

"I can't believe this is really happening," Emily whispered, leaning into Luke's side with a contented sigh. "It feels like a dream."

Luke grinned, pressing a gentle kiss to her temple. "A dream come true. God has truly blessed us, Em."

Across the room, Emily's mother caught her eye, a knowing smile on her face. "You two are absolutely meant to be," she called out. "I've never seen my girl so happy."

Emily blushed, ducking her head. "Mom, you're embarrassing me," she laughed, but the joy in her voice was unmistakable.

As the day went on, filled with festive meals and merry gift exchanges, Emily and Luke found moments to reflect on the profound love they shared. They recalled the winding paths that led them back to each other, marveling at the perfect timing of it all.

"I made a promise years ago," Emily confided as they stood by the frosted window, watching snowflakes drift lazily from the sky. "To trust in God's plan for my heart. And now, with you, I know that promise has been fulfilled."

Luke brushed a stray lock of hair from her face, his blue eyes shining with adoration. "I feel the same way, Em. You're the answer to prayers I didn't even know I was praying."

Later that evening, as the house grew quiet and the last of the guests said their goodbyes, Emily found herself drawn to the old Bible on her bookshelf. She ran her fingers over the well-worn cover, a sense of peace washing over her.

Settling into the armchair by the fading light

of the tree, she opened the pages to where she had once written her promise. The words, faded but still legible, seemed to dance before her eyes:

> Trust in the Lord with all your heart, and lean not on your own understanding; In all your ways acknowledge Him, and He shall direct your paths. — Proverbs 3:5-6

Emily closed her eyes, a silent prayer of gratitude on her lips. She thanked God for the winding road that led her here, to this moment of perfect love and understanding. For bringing Luke back into her life, a partner in faith and devotion.

And as she sat there, bathed in the soft glow of Christmas lights, Emily knew that this was just the beginning of a beautiful journey—one guided by the hand of a loving God, and sealed with the promise of a love that would last a lifetime.

EPILOGUE

The twinkling lights of the Christmas tree cast a warm glow across the room as Emily and Luke stood hand in hand, their eyes locked on each other. The gentle rustling of the tree's branches and the soft crackling of the fireplace were the only sounds that broke the comfortable silence between them.

Theirs was a beautiful wedding, held right during the Christmas season that had brought them together.

And they couldn't be happier.

"I can't believe this is real," Emily whispered, her voice filled with awe. "That we're here, together, after all these years."

Luke's lips curved into a tender smile. "God's

timing is perfect, Em. He brought us back to each other when we needed it most."

Emily nodded, leaning her head against his shoulder. "I know there will be challenges ahead, but with you by my side and God guiding us, I feel like we can face anything."

"We can," Luke affirmed, pressing a gentle kiss to her forehead. "Our love is built on a foundation of faith, and that's something that can weather any storm."

As they stood there, wrapped in each other's embrace, Emily's mind drifted to the future—to the life they would build together. She pictured lazy Sunday mornings, shared prayers over breakfast, and evenings spent in service to their community. She saw the laughter and the tears, the triumphs and the trials, all woven together by the unbreakable thread of their love.

"I can't wait to spend forever with you," she murmured, her eyes shining with unshed tears of joy.

Luke's hand came up to cradle her cheek, his thumb brushing away the single tear that escaped. "Forever and always, Em. That's the promise we made today, and it's one I intend to keep."

In that moment, standing there in the soft

light of the Christmas tree, Emily knew that this was just the beginning of their happily ever after. A story written by the hand of God, a love born of faith and sealed with the magic of the Christmas season.

And as they leaned in for a tender kiss, the world seemed to fade away, leaving only the two of them—hearts full of love, souls intertwined by destiny, ready to face whatever the future might bring, together.

EXCERPT FROM MAIDEN'S BLUSH

Terror filled her as she ran, stumbling across the snowy terrain. Her arms and legs stung from the icy wind whipping across them. She cried out as something sharp struck her. Pushing past the thorny branch, she felt the cut now upon her visage. As the tears trickled down her face, she felt the salty burn of them upon the fresh gash across her right cheek.

A roar sounded behind her, and she turned as the red Lexus skidded to a stop. A new panic seized her as she heard the door slam shut and saw the figure racing toward her. She turned and fled, faster than before, hoping she could make it to the road just ahead.

Hearing the deafening thumps of the steps

getting closer, she hazarded a look back. As she turned, the strap of one petite heel stuck on a low-lying branch, tripping her. She smashed to the frozen ground—hard. Jerking her foot from the shoe, she scrambled up, her hands stinging against the cold snow.

Halfway up, she felt a fierce tug from behind. Harsh hands gripped her waist. "Where do you think you're going?" The dark voice rasped in her ear.

She struggled, desperately trying to break away, but he was far too strong. She screamed, and his arms tightened across her body, one hand covering her mouth. She opened her mouth and sunk her teeth into his flesh as hard as she could. He cried out in pain, cursing, as she broke free.

She had barely gotten five feet away when he recaptured her. She turned, seeing the rage in his eyes.

Then, complete darkness engulfed her as she felt the blow across her face.

❄

Jack Barringer surveyed the sparkling landscape around him through the window of his dark blue

Corvette as he carefully sped along the road toward home . Despite the snowy landscape, the roads had been freshly plowed and were pretty clear.

The sky was sprinkled with stars, and the moon bathed the scenery with a picturesque glow. He turned up his radio. With the ground covered in a glittery white blanket, he could almost believe he really was in a winter wonderland. He rolled down his window for just a moment to feel the rush of the wind, deeply breathing in the cold, clear air. Ah, there was nothing like a Massachusetts winter.

It would be nice to be home for the holidays this year. Christmas was just a month away, and he had it planned to slow things down a bit and relax until the New Year. Business had been great lately. He could certainly afford to take some time off, and, besides, he needed the break.

He was among the best translators on the market, and the clientèle he served knew it. He was bilingual in six languages: Spanish, French, Italian, German, Russian, and Arabic. That's why he could do things on his terms. His father had spared no expense to ensure his son was afforded the very best education. He could still hear his cultured voice saying, "Trust me, son, this will all prove to be useful someday."

And, oh, how right he had been. Thanks to him, he had an extremely well-paying job and was allowed to travel the world at his ease. Just recently, he'd been asked if he'd ever considered giving speeches about how to achieve financial success. That would have better suited his father's expertise.

As the flurries upon his window became thicker, he clicked his windshield wipers on. If only he'd told his father how much he had appreciated everything. He was surprised to feel a sharp stab of pain at that thought. It'd been three years since his father's yacht had sunk, taking with it the only parent he'd ever known. At first, he'd been filled with helpless fury. Why his father who had been nothing but loving and kind to everyone? Why his father whose every intention had been to serve and glorify God?

He'd raged at the Almighty and pummeled him with unanswered questions until he'd finally realized that it was useless to be angry with him. After all, he was the Alpha and Omega, the beginning and the end. He had to know what he was doing. He must have a reason for all things. Jack ran a hand through his dark hair. He'd also learned that it did no good to dwell on the past either.

All memories put aside for now, he turned the next curve in happy spirits once more but then slowed as he spotted something lying on the ground on the left side of the road. He leaned forward and squinted through his window. It looked too large to be an animal—at least a domestic animal like a dog or a cat. He watched as part of the bundle jumped up and took off toward the shiny red Lexus he hadn't even noticed was there.

Warning bells began to go off in his head. What was this? He pushed his foot on the accelerator.

The door of the vehicle ahead slammed before the automobile took off down the road with a squeal.

Something wasn't right here. That man left with too much haste. Jack pulled his vehicle onto the side of the highway and stepped out.

The form upon the ground wiggled a bit as he started toward it. He heard a faint moan that sounded much like that of a woman. Wait a minute, a woman? His brows furrowed and his progress quickened. Alarm filled him as comprehension of what he had just witnessed dawned.

He knelt over the tiny body, oblivious to the wet snow seeping through his suit, and noted the red marks upon her face. Sympathy and anger imbued him. Sympathy for the poor victim. Anger at the heartless villain who would do such a thing. What man could possibly look himself in the mirror and not feel guilt over a crime such as this? How could a man ever physically hurt a woman and not feel shamed at his actions? He'd been raised to be a gentleman. Ingrained in him was the habit to treat all women with respect. He'd been taught early on never to strike a woman, even if angry. And that was one rule he'd always followed.

He squatted down and lightly touched her tiny wrist. She didn't move. She must have lost consciousness. He gently probed her joints. Nothing was broken at least. Although judging by the marks on her face, she would likely have bruises there and elsewhere.

She needed help, so of course he couldn't just leave her there. He put his arms under her and lifted her with ease, surprised at how light she was. Her long, golden hair fell away from her face and brushed his arms. She winced and cried out in pain. Her consciousness was returning. That was definitely a good sign.

Her lids shot open, revealing big blue eyes surrounded by thick lashes that cast shadows over her delicate cheeks. She screamed and struggled, her fists flying, but weakly. He barely blocked a swing to his mouth, capturing both her wrists in one hand, while still holding her with the other. "It's okay," he said soothingly. "I'm not going to hurt you.

I'm going to help you."

When she continued her vain attempt to escape, he turned her head towards him. "You're stuck out in the middle of nowhere. It's snowing, and if you don't find somewhere warm, you'll freeze to death. Trust me," he said gently. "What do you have to lose?" He wasn't sure if she understood what he was saying. She might have been in too much shock. Nevertheless, she stilled, and he carried her to his car on the side of the road.

❄

Katrina's heart pounded in her chest as the stranger secured her in the passenger seat of the Corvette and closed the door. She watched as he passed in front of the car and got in. He was tall—very tall, at least six inches taller than she was and had dark hair and eyes. He carried himself with the ease of someone who was wealthy and sophisticated. She gulped. Just like Bryan. She shook at the mere thought of him.

Bryan was her father's manager. Her father, David Weems, was a successful lawyer, and Bryan worked for him. He was her father's most trusted friend and helped him with many of his cases. She could see them now, heads bent together busily conversing, occasionally laughing and patting each other on the back. She grimaced. Her father thought of Bryan as the son he'd never had. He depended on him. He trusted him—too much.

She shivered violently. She couldn't remember ever being this cold in her life, wearing only her black evening gown and no shoes. She'd lost those in her flight. She wished she'd have had enough sense to grab her fur coat before jumping out of the car, though at the time her only thought had been to flee.

As if sensing her thoughts and sympathizing, the engine roared to life, and heat hit her face. The stranger in the driver's seat removed his coat and then reached across the car toward her. She recoiled back, eyes wide, scooting as close to the passenger-side door as she could get, prepared to jump from this car too if need be.

The man, apparently, seeing her fear, simply placed his coat on the middle console. "To warm you faster," he nodded toward the coat gently.

"Thank you," she barely managed with a lump in her throat. She took the coat and hugged it around her shoulders as the car began to move onto the road. Suddenly, a new thought struck her. Who was this man and where was he taking her? Panic seized her. What if he were just like Bryan? He'd said he would help, but so had Bryan. What if she had escaped Bryan only to end up with someone worse?

Her hands gripped the edges of her seat tightly. "Where are you taking me?" she asked, her voice shaky.

He glanced at her. "To the hospital," he answered. "I checked your joints. Nothing's broken, but you should still be checked out by professionals."

"No!" she croaked out. He momentarily took his eyes off the road to glance over at her again. "I can't go to the hospital," she fairly shook. Bryan was smart and resourceful. If she checked into a hospital, he would surely find her.

The stranger pulled the car onto the side of the road, and she stared at his huge hands as he shifted the gear in the middle of the car into park. She stared at him warily as his muscular frame turned toward her. "What's your name?" he asked.

She paused. How did she know she could trust this man? Frantic questions ran through her mind, and she licked her lips nervously, her eyes darting out the window frantically. They were in the middle of nowhere. There was nowhere for her to run. Of course, there hadn't really been anywhere for her to run when she'd jumped out of Bryan's car either. She'd just acted on instinct then.

She glanced back at the driver. He was her only means of getting help right now. He was right. If he hadn't shown up, she would have probably become even more lost than she already was and frozen to death. Looks like it was either take a chance and trust him or become a frozen statuette. She would have to trust him.

Besides, if he had intentions of hurting her, he would have acted on them already, wouldn't he?

"Katrina," she answered hesitantly, pressing closer into the seat.

He noticed the defensive gesture, and his voice softened. "I'm Jack Barringer. And I'm not going to harm you. I'm just going to take you to a hospital where you'll be properly cared for."

"I'm not going to a hospital," she stated defiantly with a hint of panic to her voice. He raised his brows and studied her. "I'm not," she repeated firmly, uncomfortable under his scrutiny but adamant in her reiteration.

He didn't question her, just started the engine. "Where are you staying? With family, at a hotel?" His steady gaze rested on her.

Her stomach plunged as the gravity of her situation fully hit her. Here she was in the middle of nowhere sitting in a car with a complete stranger and nowhere to go. No purse, no credit cards, no identification—nothing. She almost laughed at the absurdity of it all. She didn't even have any shoes. Who would have ever thought that she, Katrina Weems, the Harvard graduate, would ever have been so stupid as to screw up this bad?

Her face paled as she thought of how angry Bryan was sure to be. She could only imagine what his wrath would be like if he found her. He was probably right now rummaging through her purse. He would know even more about her than he already assuredly did. He now had her social security number, her resumes and job applications, her money, and not to mention what else. She shuddered to think of him delving in her suitcase.

Oh, why had she been so naïve as to believe that he was only doing her father a favor by coming to pick her up at the airport? Why couldn't her father have just dropped his meeting and come to get her himself? Why did she agree to take an interview in Boston instead of flying straight home to Tennessee from California? The questions kept reverberating throughout her brain when she was jerked back to the present.

"Huh?" she asked, startled.

"I was asking if you had anywhere to stay," he repeated.

She shifted uncomfortably. "Um, no, not exactly."

He flicked his turn signal on and glanced at her curiously. "No problem then. We'll just find you a hotel to spend the night in, and we'll sort through everything tomorrow."

"It's not that easy," she said nervously.

"Why not?" He frowned.

"I don't have anyone, and all of my belongings

—my purse, everything—are gone...with him," she explained uneasily.

※

He looked over at her and for the first time realized that she carried nothing but the clothes on her back. He let out a sigh of frustration. Yes, he pitied her situation, but he was definitely not feeling up to being this caliber of a rescuer. Having a big heart, he did try to help people in need. The world could be a cruel place, especially to women. This poor girl was proof of that. He felt his indignation rise again at the injustice of what he'd glimpsed. But he'd had small gestures in mind. He'd hoped to take her home to safety and be on his merry way.

So much for a relaxing vacation. Here he was stuck with a young woman who had nothing with her and was now totally dependent on him. *Why now, Lord?* Almost immediately, he realized what a jerk he was being and was chastised by his Heavenly Father. How selfish could he be? This wasn't her fault. He certainly couldn't leave her high and dry and scared as she was. God had obviously placed him there at that moment to help her, and he knew that's what he would have to do.

How was he going to do anything to help someone who didn't even have any proof of who she was, though?

She put her head in her hands, that long, golden hair falling on either side. She looked miserable, her fancy dress torn and dirty. He guessed she was a very attractive woman when not so unkempt as she was now. It was easy to imagine that a man would notice her. But what exactly had happened to put her in the state she was in now?

Compassion and remorse filled him at his selfishness. She had refused to go to the hospital. Was she afraid of being found by her attacker? What exactly had occurred by the time he arrived on the scene? She had nowhere to go. No friends or family in the area, no hotel reservation. Had she been staying with this man? Or was it something else? He hadn't pressed her for answers. She'd been through a trying ordeal.

No, she didn't want to be in this predicament any more than he did. It was worse on her part. She was the one who had been assaulted and left out in the cold with nothing.

"Hey," he steadied the wheel with one hand and reached out to touch her shoulder with the other. Mistake. She jumped at the contact, and he winced, mumbling an apology. She physically gathered herself together and raised her head, looking like a lost little girl. It went straight to his heart. "It's going to be okay. I'll pay for each of us a room. We'll sort through everything in the morning." He smiled. "I had planned to stay a night in Boston before returning home anyway."

She looked at him with skepticism and apprehension before slowly nodding her head. "Thank you," she weakly managed before looking back down as if she were ashamed.

Get Maiden's Blush now!

ABOUT THE AUTHOR

Award-winning author Kayla Lowe writes women's fiction that explores complex themes with sensitivity and depth. Kayla's books delve into the intricacies of relationships, self-discovery, and resilience. From cozy love stories interspersed with a bit of faith to heartwarming tales of friendship and suspenseful novels of empowerment and heartbreak, her books illustrate the struggles specific to women.

When she's not churning out her next novel, you can find her with her feet in the sand and a book in her hand or curled up on the couch with her dogs.

Visit her website at www.authorkaylalowe.com.

ALSO BY KAYLA LOWE

Series

Women of the Bible Fiction

Ruth

Esther

Rachel

Hannah

Deborah

❄

Charms of the Chaste Court

A Courtship in Covent Garden

Whispers in Westminster

Romance in Regent's Park

Serenade on Strand Street

Treasure in Tower Bridge

❄

Sweet Honey by the Sea

The Beekeeper's Secret (Book 1)

A Royal Honeycomb (Book 2)

Bees in Blossom (Book 3)

Honeyed Kisses (Book 4)

Blooming Forever (Book 5)

❄

Strawberry Beach Series

Beachside Lessons (Book 1)

Beachside Lessons (Book 2)

Beachside Lessons (Book 3)

❄

Panama City Beach Series

Sun-Kissed Secrets (Book 1)

Sun-Kissed Secrets (Book 2)

Sun-Kissed Secrets (Book 3)

❄

The Tainted Love Saga

Of Love and Deception (Book 1)

Of Love and Family (Book 2)

Of Love and Violence (Book 3)

Of Love and Abuse (Book 4)

Of Love and Crime (Book 5)

Of Love and Addiction (Book 6)

Of Love and Redemption (Book 7)

❄

<u>Standalones</u>

Maiden's Blush

❄

<u>Poetry</u>

Phantom Poetry

Lost and Found